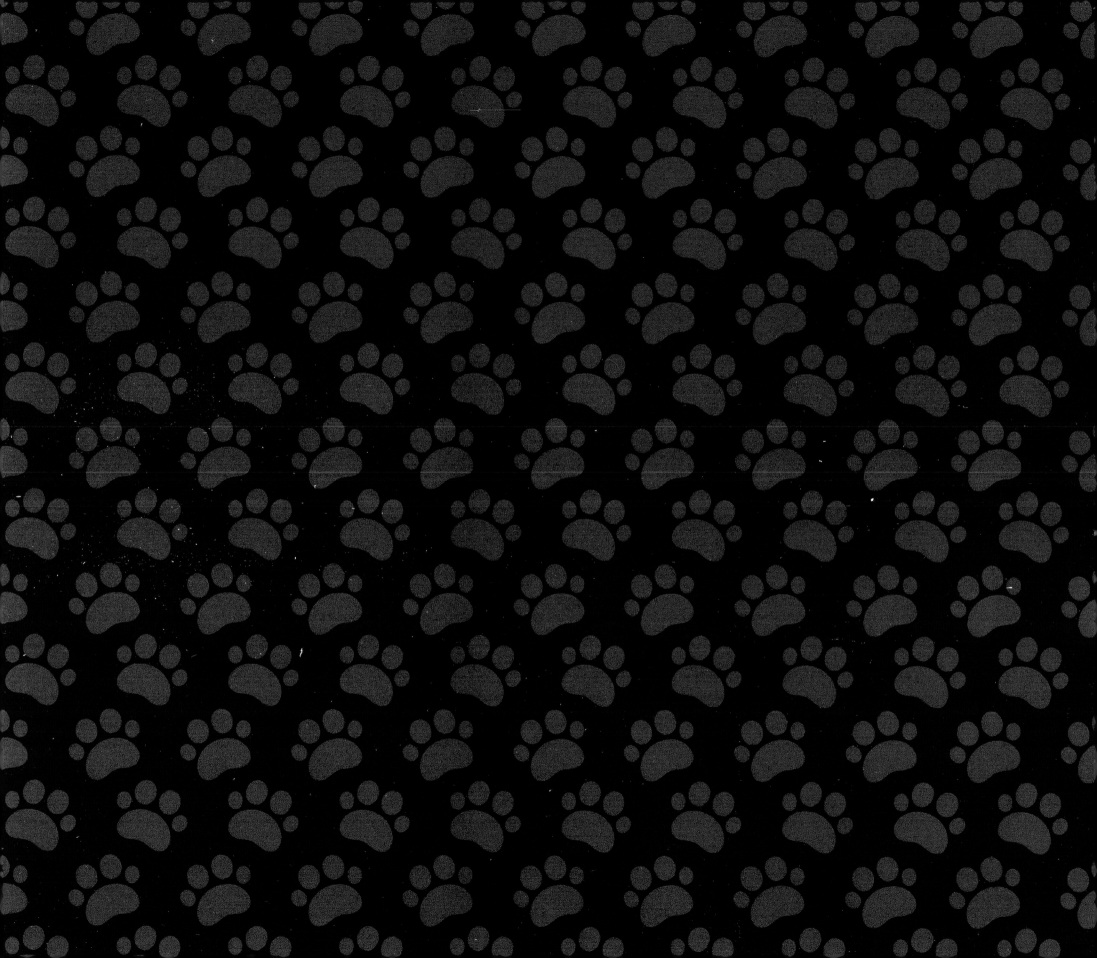

ADVENTURE TED

NIGHT AT THE ENCHANTED THEME PARK

Created by Tommy Head | Illustrations by Joel Cockrell

To Mom & Dad,

Thank you for always helping me to see the
adventure in all that I do.

Love,

It was a dark, stormy night.

The wind was howling and the floors were creaking.

Everyone was fast asleep, except one little boy who lay in his room—wide awake, and uneasy about something.

It was going to be a long night.

Suddenly, the thunder cracked, the skies opened, and the rain began to pour.

"Make it stop!" shouted Timmy.

But then, Timmy noticed what appeared to be a shiny necklace, hanging from a tree branch near his window.

"How strange," he mumbled.

"I wonder how that got there," he said as he began to approach the window, cautiously.

As he reached for the dangling necklace, there was a loud roar of thunder.

Timmy quickly grabbed it and dove back into his bed like a rabbit, pulling the covers over his head.

Under the covers, Timmy examined the necklace.

He contemplated waking his parents, but he had already done so every night that week and he knew they were very tired.

Clutching the necklace, he plead again: "Please, if anyone can hear me, make it stop!"

All of a sudden, a tiny aircraft soared through the window.

It crashed against Timmy's dresser and skidded across the floor.

A cloud of smoke filled the room, and through the haze Timmy noticed something strange about the aircraft.

It was growing! Originally the size of a shoebox, it had now grown even larger than Timmy's bed!

As a small door on the side of the aircraft began to open, a radiant light shone through.

Squinting through the brightness, Timmy noticed something standing in the doorway—or was it some*one*?

He moved closer to get a better look.

It was a teddy bear!

Timmy cautiously approached the teddy bear, when all of a sudden it looked up at him and said,

"Hello there! Sorry for the rough landing; the weather is terrible tonight! My name is Adventure Ted, but you can call me Ted for short. How do you do?"

Timmy was stunned. Confused, he asked, "You can talk?"

"Oh, yes, and much, much more!" responded Ted. "But for now, how can I help you?"

"What do you mean?" Timmy asked, puzzled.

"Well, I got your message," Ted explained. "Anyone who has a Ted Tag—the necklace you're holding there—can reach me when they really need to."

Ted held up a controller and replayed Timmy's message wishing for the rain to stop.

"Not a big fan of the rain, I see. Where are your parents?" asked Ted.

"They're asleep in their room, but I don't want to bother them again. They are very tired," Timmy sullenly explained. "We've been going to the doctor a lot lately, and tomorrow we have to go to the hospital early in the morning."

"Say no more; Adventure Ted is here!" exclaimed Ted with his hands on his hips.

"You can stop the rain?" Timmy asked, hopefully.

"Not exactly," Ted explained, "but I can take you somewhere special– to wait out the storm, and help ease your mind. A change of scenery can really help in these types of situations. Now, if I can just find my…"

Timmy watched as Ted dug around in his Adventure Pack, almost disappearing inside.

"A-ha!" he exclaimed, revealing a huge spare propeller. "Once we replace the propeller on the Adventure Craft, it'll be good as new!" Waving Timmy over, Ted asked, "Can you please give me a hand with this, Timmy?"

"Sure!" Timmy replied.

"Thanks for your help, Timmy!" exclaimed Ted, tightening up the last bolt on the propeller. "Now watch this!" Ted took out his controller and pushed a button.

Suddenly, the Adventure Craft beamed a ray of light against the wall, creating a vortex.

"Let's go on an adventure and get out of this rainy town until the storm passes. Sound good?" asked Ted.

Timmy nodded.

"Well then, follow me!" exclaimed Ted.

ADVENTURE HUNT 1

On this page, find a wrench, a paw print,
and the Adventure Ted badge.

Need help? Visit *AdventureTedWorld.com* for the answer key.

Timmy joined Ted in the cockpit. Sitting side by side, they gazed into the portal.

"Welcome aboard the Adventure Craft, Timmy, where there are no limits, and anything is possible," Ted said with a smile, turning to his new co-pilot.

"Don't forget to buckle up!"
cautioned Ted, pulling his goggles
down over his eyes.

Then, with the click of Timmy's
seatbelt, the Adventure Craft
launched forward into the portal.

"Wooohooooo!" exclaimed Ted.
"The adventure has begun!"

As they traveled through the interdimensional portal, Timmy was awestruck by the tunnel of swirling colors and lights. It was unlike anything he had ever seen before.

"Nearly there!" announced Ted.

"Try to land a little more smoothly than last time," Timmy joked.

ADVENTURE HUNT 2

On this page, find a paw print, the Adventure Ted badge, and a face.

Need help? Visit *AdventureTedWorld.com* for the answer key.

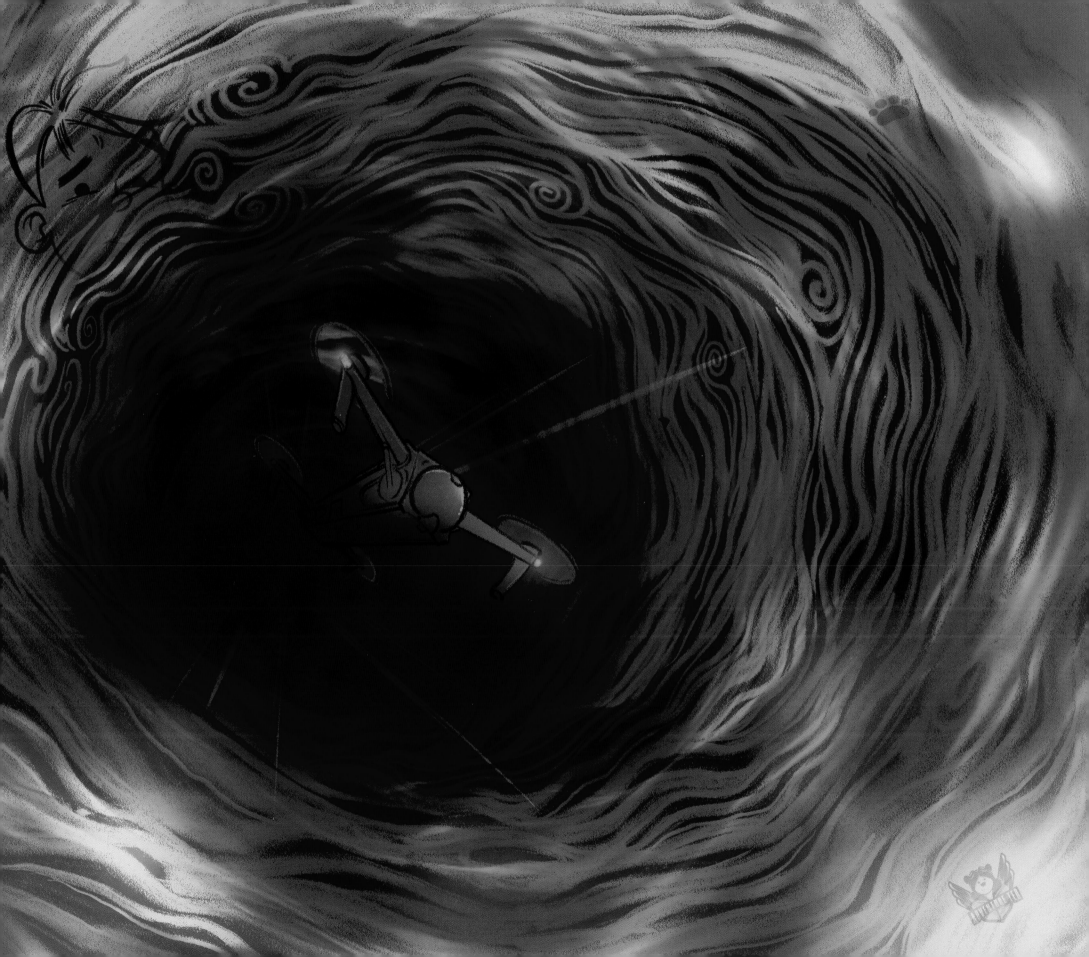

Once through the portal, Ted landed the Adventure Craft safely and the two exited through the same doorway where Timmy first spotted Ted.

Except, this time, they weren't in Timmy's bedroom.

"Welcome to The Enchanted Theme Park, fellas! I'm Park Keeper Rick," said a friendly man at the entrance. "You sure are in for a treat! There are no lines here, so get in there and enjoy as many rides as you can!"

Overwhelmed with excitement, Timmy and Ted sprinted through the park's gates to embark on the adventure of a lifetime!

Next, Timmy and Ted walked to Chef Otto's restaurant, the Octo Diner, for a bite to eat.

"Hello Mr. Ted! And, who do we have here?" asked Chef Otto.

"This is Timmy, one of our newest Adventurers," replied Ted.

"It's a pleasure to meet you, Timmy," said Otto. "And congratulations on becoming an Adventurer! I hope you guys are hungry. I've prepared a special feast for the two of you."

"Thank you, Chef Otto!" replied Timmy, excited to dig in.
While enjoying the spectacular feast, Ted and Timmy discussed the night.

"Did you enjoy the Sky Coaster?" asked Ted.

"I did!" replied Timmy. "Although, I'm not a big fan of the upside-down parts."

"You know," said Ted, "life is a lot like a roller coaster."

"Really? How?" asked Timmy.

"Well like a roller coaster, life has its ups and downs—and even its upside-downs!" Ted explained. "There are good parts, and then there are parts you may not like so much. But always remember, it's all part of the ride. Getting through the tough parts is always easier when you know that the good parts are just around the corner."

After dinner, Timmy and Ted boarded the Adventure Craft and returned home.

"Thanks for a great time, Ted," said Timmy. "This really helped me take my mind off tomorrow. I almost forgot that I'm going to the hospital."

"My pleasure! You see, Timmy, life is just one big adventure with infinite possibilities. It is true, some parts are scary, but others are amazing! You can't appreciate the good without experiencing the bad sometimes. The key is to see the adventure in all that you do, and understand that those bumpy parts are just part of the journey to the best parts."

"Thanks, Ted. I'm really glad I met you," said Timmy. "By the way, here is your Ted Tag. Thanks for letting me borrow it."

"I want you to keep it, Timmy," said Ted. "You are now a fellow Adventurer! Until we meet again, let it remind you to see the adventure in all that you do."

"Also, I have a little something for you to use while you're waiting around at the hospital," said Ted, pulling a video game console out of his Adventure Pack.

"You'll be fine tomorrow," Ted promised Timmy.

"Remember, you are an Adventurer now. Be brave for your parents, and soon we will meet again for another adventure."

"I will! Thank you for everything!" Timmy exclaimed, giving Ted a big hug.

"I'll see you soon!" said Ted.

Ted returned to the Adventure Craft, took off, and flew back out through the window.

After a restful sleep, Timmy woke up to a beautiful sunny morning. The smell of French toast and cinnamon filled the house.

He marched downstairs, feeling confident and prepared for the day ahead.

"Are you ready for today, kiddo?" asked Timmy's dad.

"Let's get this adventure going!" replied Timmy, surprising his parents with his positive attitude.

At the hospital, Timmy was surprised how pleasant everything was. There were decorations on the walls, fun games to play, and other kids his age in the waiting room.

Eventually, the nurse called Timmy's name. "Timmy?" she asked, looking around the waiting room.

Timmy threw his hand up in the air and exclaimed, "I'm over here!"

ADVENTURE HUNT 3

On this page, find a toy spaceship, a paw print, and the Adventure Ted badge.

Need help? Visit *AdventureTedWorld.com* for the answer key.

Timmy's doctor entered the room. "Ready, Timmy? Everything is going to be okay," he said, pointing to a badge on his coat.

"Adventure Ted!" Timmy thought to himself, assuming his doctor and Ted must know one another.

Timmy remained brave, remembering Ted's lessons from the previous night.

During his hospital visit, Timmy enjoyed the new gaming console that Ted had given to him the night before.

As he played, he smiled while thinking about Ted and their exciting adventure together. Meanwhile, Timmy's parents stood next to him, beaming with pride over his bravery.

His mom whispered, "I am so proud of him."
Dad agreed, "Me too."

Through the window, Adventure Ted watched from afar, making sure that everything went smoothly.
He too was proud of Timmy—for being brave and overcoming his fears, like a true Adventurer.

The End

"No matter where you are, or with whom,
see the adventure in all that you do!"

———

Adventure Ted

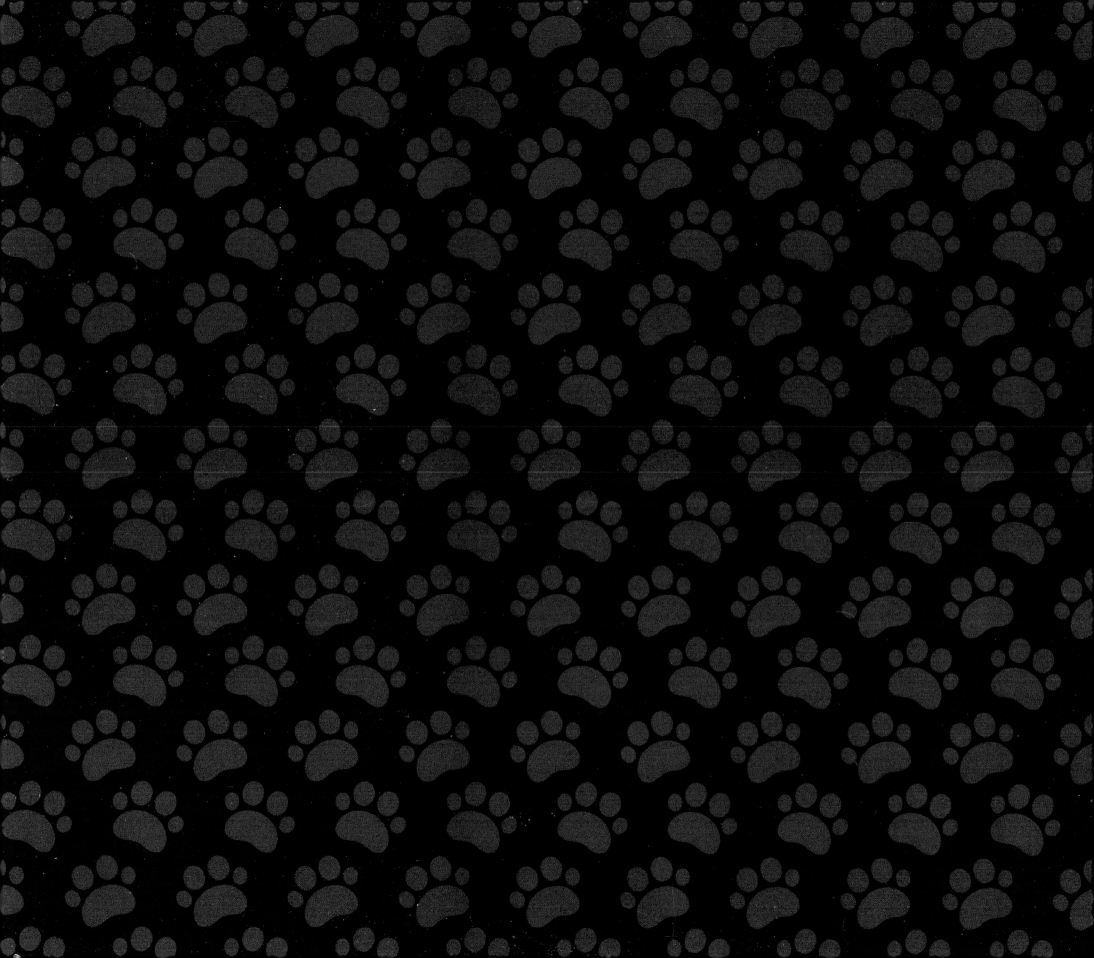